The Presbyterian Church in
Ireland
League of Church Loyalty

This Prize

was awarded to

Andrew Byrne

for

Regular Attendance at Church during

year 1991

_____ Minister

_____ Secretary

ISBN 0-86163-223-0

Copyright © 1988 Award Publications Limited

Original story first published 1911
This edition first published 1988

Third Impression 1990

Published by Award Publications Limited
Spring House, Spring Place,
Kentish Town, London NW5 3BH

Printed in Hungary

PETER PAN
AND WENDY

Illustrated
by
Anne Grahame Johnstone

Adapted for young children
from J.M. Barrie's original text
by Jane Carruth

AWARD PUBLICATIONS LIMITED
LONDON

CONTENTS

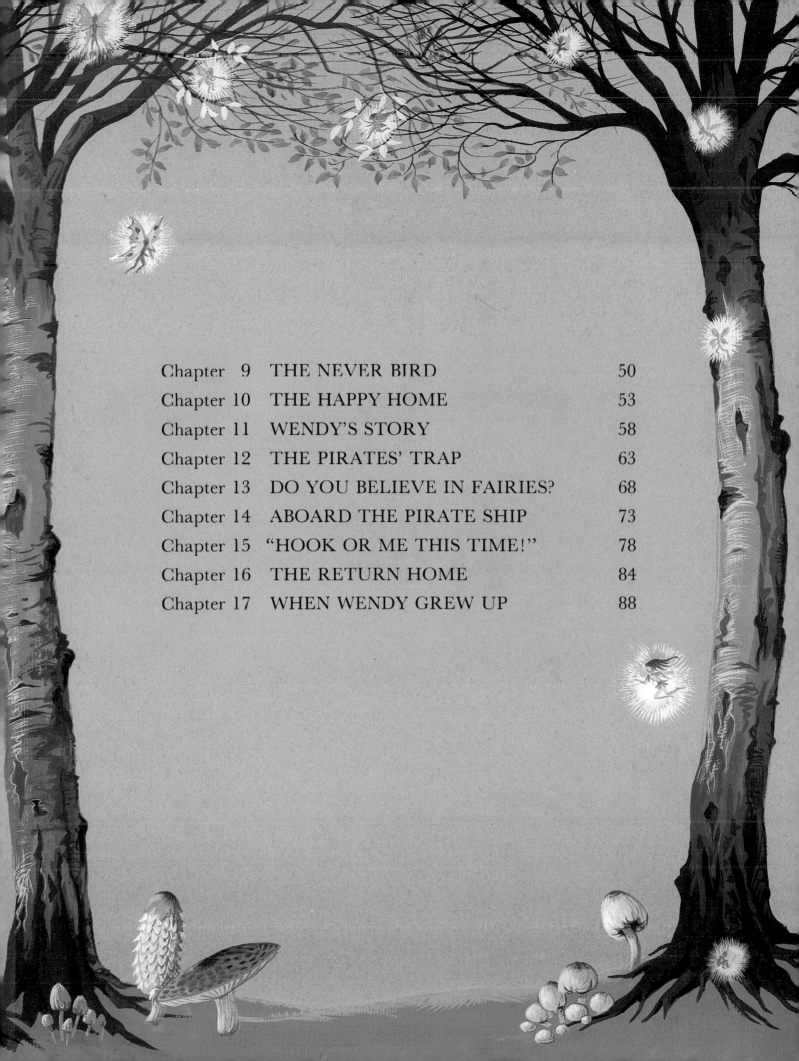

1   PETER BREAKS THROUGH

Everybody knows that children have to grow up. Wendy had known this for ages. But she didn't think much about it until she met Peter Pan!

Wendy lived with her mother and father, Mr. and Mrs. Darling, and her two brothers, in a tall house in London. Wendy was first. Then came John, then Michael.

Mrs. Darling was a pretty, romantic lady who loved her children. Mr. Darling loved his children too, but not quite in the same way, because he was always worrying about money.

The nurse taking care of his children was not exactly the nurse Mr. Darling would have wished for, but she was all he could afford. She was a prim Newfoundland dog called Nana who had belonged to no one in particular until the Darlings had come across her in Kensington Gardens and engaged her.

Nana proved herself a treasure. She could tell at a glance when any of her charges was genuinely ill. And if Mrs. Darling brought unexpected visitors to the nursery, Nana had Michael dressed in his best pinafore and his hair smoothed out seconds before they reached the nursery door.

Now, like all proper nurses, Nana had one night off in the week, and it was on these nights that Mrs. Darling took her place in the nursery.

Sometimes, before it was time to be tucked up in bed, Wendy would speak about the Neverland, their secret magic island where, she told her mother, she had a wolf for a pet. John said there was a fantastic lagoon on the island with flamingoes flying over it.

"I live in a house made of leaves on the island," Wendy told her. "And Peter comes to visit me . . . ."

Once Mrs. Darling had asked about Peter.

"Who is he, my dear?"

"He is Peter Pan. You know, mother," Wendy had said. "He isn't grown up and he can fly! Sometimes he comes into the nursery and sits at the foot of my bed and plays his pipes!"

Mrs. Darling remained puzzled and upset by this conversation. She tried to remember if she had ever heard or read about a boy called Peter Pan. At last she seemed to recall that he was said to live with the fairies.

On some nights when Mrs. Darling kept watch in the nursery she settled down quietly by the fire without any disturbing thoughts. But on this particular night she kept glancing around the cosy room. The familiar toys, Michael's Noah's ark and the favourite, faithful rocking horse, the dolls' house and the books — they were all comforting. Still she felt restless and uneasy until she took up her sewing.

Presently, as she sat quietly stitching, her head began to nod. Then, gently, oh so gently, she fell fast asleep and while she slept she had a dream.

In her dream the mysterious Neverland — the Neverland Wendy sometimes talked about — had come too near. There was that strange boy. He, too, had come near. It was as if he had broken free of the Neverland to come and visit her!

Then, as she went on dreaming, the window of the nursery suddenly blew open and a boy did drop on the floor.

This strange boy was not alone. With him was a bright light, quite dazzling but no bigger than a fist, which darted about the room like a living thing. I think it must have been this bright light which wakened Mrs. Darling.

She started up with a cry. When she saw the handsome boy something told her who he was. Peter Pan! He was dressed in leaves but looked in some way quite ordinary! Mrs. Darling stared and stared at him, and Peter Pan, to show how much he disliked grown-ups, made a horrid face at her which greatly upset the poor lady.

2 THE SHADOW

You can hardly blame Mrs. Darling for screaming! She screamed and screamed and as if in answer to her screams the nursery door was violently flung open and in came Nana who was back from her night out.

Nana paid no attention to Mrs. Darling. With a deep, angry growl, she rushed at the strange boy who had dared to invade her nursery. But Peter Pan was too quick for her. In one graceful movement he sprang lightly to the window and then through it.

Now the nursery was three floors up, at the very top of the tall house, and Mrs. Darling, fearing that the pretty boy had leapt to his death, left the room and ran down the stairs into the street to search for his poor little body. But, of course, it was not there! When she looked up into the black sky she saw nothing but what she took to be a shooting star!

On returning to the nursery she saw Nana with something in her mouth. It was the boy's shadow! As he leapt through the window Nana had slammed it shut. She was too late to catch him but Peter's shadow had not been able to escape.

Mrs. Darling took the shadow and rolled it up carefully. Then she put it away in a drawer until she could tell her husband all about her strange visitor.

A whole week passed before Mrs. Darling had a chance to speak to her husband about the unusual events which had taken place in the nursery.

It was on a Friday, and the evening had begun in the most ordinary way imaginable. In fact it was a Friday just like any other Friday!

Nana had run the water for Michael's bath. Michael, as he did every bath night, had protested loudly that he did not want a bath. Of course Nana would not put up with such nonsense! As usual she had carried Michael on her back into the bathroom. And just as usual Michael had shouted and kicked and made a fuss.

Afterwards Mrs. Darling had come into the nursery in her charming white evening dress which was one of Wendy's favourites. "Your father and I are going out to dinner at No.27," she told the children. "So we won't be far away."

Just at that moment Mr. Darling rushed into the nursery holding a crumpled tie. "I simply can't tie this beastly tie!" he shouted, clearly in a very bad mood. "I'm warning you — unless I get it fixed we won't be going out to dinner."

"Let me try, dear," said his wife calmly. In no time at all her nimble fingers had fixed the wayward tie.

Mr. Darling's black mood cleared and Mrs. Darling was beginning to wonder if she could possibly begin telling him about the strange boy and his lost shadow. She was on the point when into the room came Nana and as ill luck would have it Mr. Darling brushed quite violently against her. Of course it wasn't Nana's fault but Mr. Darling's brand new trousers, the smartest he had ever worn, were covered with her long hairs. Of course Mrs. Darling brushed away the hairs at once but her husband was so annoyed that he began saying, not for the first time, that it was a sad mistake to have a dog for a nurse!

"George, Nana is a treasure!" Mrs. Darling cried indignantly. And then she began telling him about Peter Pan. Mr. Darling laughed at the whole story but when he saw the shadow he looked more thoughtful. And he was still thoughtful when Nana appeared again, this time with Michael's medicine.

Now Mr. Darling was always trying to impress his children and so when Michael positively refused his medicine, he remarked loudly, "When I was your age I took my medicine without any fuss . . . ."

The real truth was that Mr. Darling hated taking medicine and had hidden his own special brand on the top of the wardrobe! Wendy, wanting to be helpful, quickly found the bottle and brought it to her father. Now he was trapped! But still

he couldn't bring himself to take the foul stuff. So, to save face, he poured it into Nana's bowl, at the same time laughing loudly, hoping his children would think it a splendid joke!

The joke fell flat especially when Nana came in and lapped up the horrid medicine. Mr. Darling was deeply ashamed, but to show that he was still the master he banished poor Nana to the yard — kennel and all!

In the meantime Mrs. Darling had put the children to bed. They could hear Nana barking and Wendy said, "That is Nana's special bark when she smells danger!"

"Are you sure, Wendy?" Mrs. Darling asked, and she shivered. Then she went to the window and made sure it was securely fastened, saying, "The sky is peppered with beautiful stars tonight," as she left the nursery.

Of course stars are beautiful
and like to be admired, but they
are not always friendly. They
were not really friendly towards
Peter and that night they wanted
to see some fun. So, as soon as
the grown-ups were out of the
way, they told Peter the road was
clear. In fact it was the smallest
of all the stars that screamed out,
"Now, Peter!" A cry which sent
Peter and Tinker Bell on their
way to the nursery.

3   COME AWAY! COME AWAY!

It was quiet and still in the big nursery until, all at once, there darted into the room a tiny ball of light. It was Tinker Bell, the little fairy girl who followed Peter wherever he chanced to go. Then, a moment later, the window was blown wide open with the help of the little stars who breathed on it, and Peter himself dropped on to the nursery floor.

"Tinker Bell, Tinker Bell," Peter whispered. "Do you know where my shadow is? I expect you do and you must tell me! You know I must have my shadow!"

Tinker Bell answered him in her own fairy language which, to ordinary mortals, sounded just like the tinkle of golden bells. Of course Peter understood her perfectly. "Your shadow is in the big box over there!" she told him.

Peter knew she was really describing the big solid chest of drawers. He went over to it and there was his beloved shadow in one of the drawers!

In his pleasure and excitement in finding his shadow Peter forgot all about his little friend, Tinker Bell. He shut the drawer quickly without troubling to find out what Tinker Bell was doing. And, oh dear, he shut her inside the drawer!

Of course all Peter was thinking about was how to make his shadow stick on. When it wouldn't stick by itself, he tried to stick it with soap from the bathroom, but that failed.

He was so bitterly disappointed that he sat down on the floor and began to cry. It was simply a dreadful thing not to have a shadow!

Peter's sobs soon woke Wendy and she sat up in bed, not in the least frightened to find a strange boy on the nursery floor. "Why are you crying?" she asked at once. Then she went on, "By the way, I'm Wendy. Wendy Moira Angela Darling . . . ."

"And I'm Peter Pan," Peter told her. "And I'm crying because I can't get my shadow to stick on. It has come off!"

"It certainly won't stick with soap," Wendy exclaimed. "But I know how to make it stick. It will have to be sewn on with needle and thread."

Peter looked puzzled and so Wendy began explaining about stitching things together as she jumped out of bed and got her work basket.

"It might hurt a little," she went on, kneeling down beside him. "But not much . . . ."

"I don't mind," said Peter, clenching his teeth. "I shan't cry." But he kept his teeth firmly clenched until the shadow was sewn on.

Wendy offered to give him a kiss for being brave. But, on finding out that he didn't know about kisses, she gave him a thimble instead. And Peter, not to be outdone, gave her an acorn button.

Then Peter told her about the beginning of fairies and how when the first baby laughed, its laugh broke into a thousand pieces, and they all went skipping about and that was the beginning of fairies.

Talking about fairies made him remember Tinker Bell. And suddenly he heard her. "I do believe I've shut Tink in the drawer!" he laughed. And so he had!

As soon as he let poor Tinker Bell out of the drawer she flew about the nursery screaming with fury. But Peter only laughed louder. "I've said I am sorry," was all the apology he would make.

Tinker Bell was anxious to fly back to the Neverland. But Peter wanted to stay and talk to Wendy. "I used to come to your window to listen to your stories," he told her. "In the Neverland where I come from there are some lost boys — boys who have no mothers — who would love your stories. You could darn their socks too and cook for them and be their mother. They would love you . . . and I would teach you to fly . . . ."

"Could John and Michael come too?" Wendy asked, thinking how wonderful it would be to fly.

"I suppose so," said Peter. "If you wake them up I'll teach you all to fly."

Wendy shook her brothers awake and when she told them about flying, they were as excited as she was. Peter blew fairy dust all over them and told them to wriggle their shoulders.

Then he shouted, "Come! Follow me!"
And he soared out of the window — away into the night with Wendy, John and Michael close behind.

4   THE FLIGHT

It was certainly wonderful fun flying through the star lit sky. John, for no reason at all, wore his very own top hat which he treasured and little Michael clutched his toy rabbit. Wendy had brought nothing of her own to remind her of the nursery. That didn't bother her. But sometimes as the boys raced each other or flew in circles, she wondered if Peter really knew where they were going.

"Second to the right and straight on till morning," Peter had told her, describing the position of the Neverland. But they didn't always seem to be flying straight!

Once Peter left them to have an adventure of his own.
When he returned, he told them the Neverland was close and
he called out in his captain's voice, "We get off here!" In fact
they had been making straight for it all the time, not so
much thanks to Peter but because the island itself was
looking out for them!

Wendy and John and Michael stood on tiptoe in the air

Wild Beasts

The Fairies

Home U

The Redskins' Camp

The Crocodile

24

to get their first sight of the magic island, and, strange to say, they all recognised it at once.

John recognised the lagoon and the old boat. Wendy pointed out the redskin camp and the wolf with her cubs and so many other familiar things. It was like returning home for the holidays. Of course in those days the Neverland had been make-believe!

Ye MAPPE of the NEVERLAND or PETER PAN'S ISLAND

Wendy's House

Michael's Wigwam

John's Boat

...round

Marooners' Rock

The Never Bird

The Mermaids' Lagoon

Mysterious River

Kidd's Creek

Jolly Roger

The Neverland was real now and their nursery seemed a thousand miles away. Where was Nana? Somehow memories of brave Nana pushed themselves into their thoughts as they began flying low over the island for now it had suddenly grown hostile and threatening. There was no visible enemy, but it seemed as if they were pushing against an invisible force — a force so strong that it made them hang in the air. Even Peter looked serious especially when he had to beat against the air with his fists to help them move forward.

"They don't want us to land," he explained. And Wendy shivered. "Why not?" she asked.

But Peter refused to tell her. Instead he sent Tinker Bell on ahead to spy out the land. When she returned she spoke rapidly and Peter translated. "The pirates have already sighted us," he said. "They've got out their big gun, Long Tom. They'll shoot us down . . . ."

"They certainly will if they spot Tinker Bell's bright light," John cried. "She'll give us all away!"

"Well, she can't put out her light," Peter said. "It only goes out when she falls asleep. And I won't send her away." Then he laughed. "I've just had a brilliant idea. She could travel in your hat, John. What do you say?"

Tinker Bell had no objection to hiding away in John's hat. She hoped very much, of course, that Peter would volunteer to carry it. When he didn't it was left to John to offer.

Presently John gave Wendy the hat because he found he couldn't fly so well when carrying it. Now that did make the fairy absolutely furious. She hated accepting favours from Wendy!

5 THE ISLAND COME TRUE

Meanwhile on the island itself Peter's boys were out searching for their leader, armed to the teeth and determined to defend themselves to the death should they encounter their dreaded enemy, the pirates!

Prepared for anything, the gallant band moved in single file through the dark forest.

The pirates, under the leadership of Captain James Hook, were a villainous bunch of desperate men. But not one of them matched the dreadful cruelty of their captain.

In appearance Hook had a foppish look, favouring plumed hats and heavily brocaded coats. His long black hair was always dressed in tight corkscrew curls and he was rarely seen without the two cigars which he smoked at the same time in a holder of his own invention. But the most terrifying and memorable part of him was his iron claw.

If you dared ask him about his claw he might or might not tell you how he fought the boy, Peter Pan, who cut off his right arm and fed it to a passing crocodile. Then he might go on to tell you of his terrible fear of that same crocodile which now pursued him day and night over land and sea, licking its lips for the rest of him!

"So it would have had me by now," he would most likely add, "had it not swallowed a clock which goes tick-tick inside it and so warns me of its approach!"

The lost boys knew the story of Hook and the crocodile and often laughed over it. But now as the boys continued the search for their leader, they could only hope that neither Hook nor the crocodile was anywhere near.

Now, one of the other boys, Nibs, was in the lead as they left the shelter of the trees. And it was he who first spotted a great white bird flying their way.

By now Tinker Bell was almost overhead.

"Hello, Tink," Nibs called out in astonishment. "Where is Peter?"

"He's coming," Tinker Bell cried. "But now you must shoot down the Wendy bird. It's what Peter wishes!"

Poor jealous Tinker Bell! She was now quite determined to destroy Wendy before Peter grew to like her so much that he made her stay forever on their island. Now she had found a way for she had managed to separate Wendy from the others as they flew along.

"We must do what Peter wishes," the boys cried. "Bows and arrows! Bows and arrows at the ready!" But only one of the boys had a bow and arrows, and, urged on by Tink, Tootles fitted an arrow to his bow and then fired, and Wendy fluttered to the ground with an arrow in her breast.

"I have shot the Wendy bird!" Tootles cried proudly. But as the other boys crowded round Wendy a terrible silence fell upon the wood.

Tootles looked about him like a conqueror until one of the other boys exclaimed, "This is no bird! I — I think it must be a lady!" And his voice shook.

"A lady!" Tootles cried aghast.

Poor Tootles — he was trembling as he spoke. "I dare not face Peter!" But as he moved away, they heard a sound which made their hearts stand still. It was Peter's own special sound — a loud crow to warn them he was near. Again came that ringing crow and then he dropped in front of them.

"Great news, boys!" he cried. "I have brought you a mother!"

Tootles turned back. "Peter, the boys are trying to hide her from you. But she is there — lying on the ground — shot by my arrow!"

Peter knelt down by Wendy and took the arrow from her heart. And wonder of wonders — she opened her eyes. "She lives," he said shortly. "The arrow did not pierce her heart but struck the acorn button I once gave her. It is the kiss I gave her. It saved her life!"

The boys cheered and clapped their hands until one of them cried, "Just listen to Tinker Bell — she is sobbing because the Wendy lives!"

Then they told him how Tink had persuaded Tootles to fire his arrow.

In a sudden burst of anger, Peter shouted, "I am your friend no more, Tink! Begone from me!"

He turned his attention to Wendy who lay very still on the ground. "She is too weak to be carried down into our house," one of the boys remarked.

"But if she lies there she will die," Tootles said.

"We must build a little house around her," Peter cried. "That is what we must do. But first we must invite the doctor to come and see her. . . ."

As he spoke John and Michael dropped out of the sky almost at his feet. How relieved they were to see Peter again!

"What's Wendy doing down there?" John asked presently.

"She needs a doctor," Peter said seriously, and he turned to one of the boys. "You're her doctor! You should be wearing your doctor's hat . . . ."

The boy knew better than to protest. In a moment he had snatched John's hat and put it on his own head. Now he was ready to be the very wise, clever doctor Peter expected him to be, even though it was only make-believe!

The forest rang with the sound of axes as the boys cut down branches for the building of the little house. Soon, almost everything needed for a cosy dwelling lay at Wendy's feet.

"I wish we knew what kind of house she really wants," Tootles said at last.

"Perhaps she'll tell us as she sleeps," said Peter. And immediately without opening her eyes Wendy began to sing:

"I wish I had a pretty house
The littlest ever seen
With funny little red walls
And roof of mossy green."

The boys were delighted when they heard this for by the greatest good luck the branches they had brought were sticky with red sap and all the ground was carpeted with moss.

The little house grew and grew around Wendy and it was really quite beautiful. Everybody was delighted until Peter said,

"There's no chimney. We must have a chimney!" Then he grabbed John's hat, knocked out the bottom and put the hat on the roof!

The hat made an excellent chimney and everybody declared themselves well satisfied. So did Wendy, the new owner of this beautiful little house.

Peter was the first to knock politely on the door, and when Wendy answered his knock and stood in the doorway, all the boys saluted her politely. Then Peter told her all that had happened.

Wendy insisted on putting all the lost boys to bed in their own underground house. Then she returned to her little house under the trees and Peter kept watch outside with drawn sword.

7 THE HOME UNDER THE GROUND:

The next day Peter explained to Wendy and her brothers that they must each have a hollow tree of their own.

"Your tree must fit you exactly," he said. "It will be the entrance above ground to our home under the ground!"

John and Michael thought it was a great way to enter a house, for once you had fitted yourself into the tree you drew in your breath at the top and down you slid at the right speed! And they soon found the right trees.

It didn't take them long to go up and down as smoothly as any of the other boys and they grew to love their underground home — especially when Wendy gathered them all together and told them one of her special stories.

The great bed was tilted against the wall by day and let down at night. All the boys except Michael slept in it. Michael should have used it but Wendy insisted that she must have a *real* baby. Michael was the littlest so he had to agree to be hung up in a basket!

Tinker Bell had her own private apartment in the big room; it was a small niche — a little alcove in the wall — shut off from the rest of the home by tiny curtains and most exquisitely furnished. Even the queen of the fairies could not have had a more delightful boudoir with the fruit-blossom bedspread so tastefully spread over the Queen Mab bed. In fact everything in the room was in the very best taste, and most of the furniture quite rare. The chandelier especially was Tinker Bell's pride and joy as was the wash stand made of pie crust!

Of course, Tinker Bell, being so jealous of Wendy, would have nothing to do with her. But this did not worry Wendy. She was so busy being a mother to the boys that there were days when she didn't find time to go above ground. Sometimes Peter ordered make-believe food but mostly Wendy cooked good nourishing food for her children, though it was not always easy to tell which was real and which was make-believe!

Sometimes when all the work was done, Peter said he would tell the bedtime story for a change. Wendy liked the one about the Never bird best of all.

All the birds were Peter's friends but the Never bird was
something special. "This year," Peter said, "she built her nest
in the branch of a tree overhanging the lagoon, and laid her
eggs in it, but then the branch broke and the nest fell into
the water."

Whenever Peter got to this part of the story Wendy would
gasp and look upset. But then Peter would say quickly, "Of
course I gave orders that the Never bird must not be
disturbed. She was to be left in peace to sit on her eggs as the
nest floated in the water!"

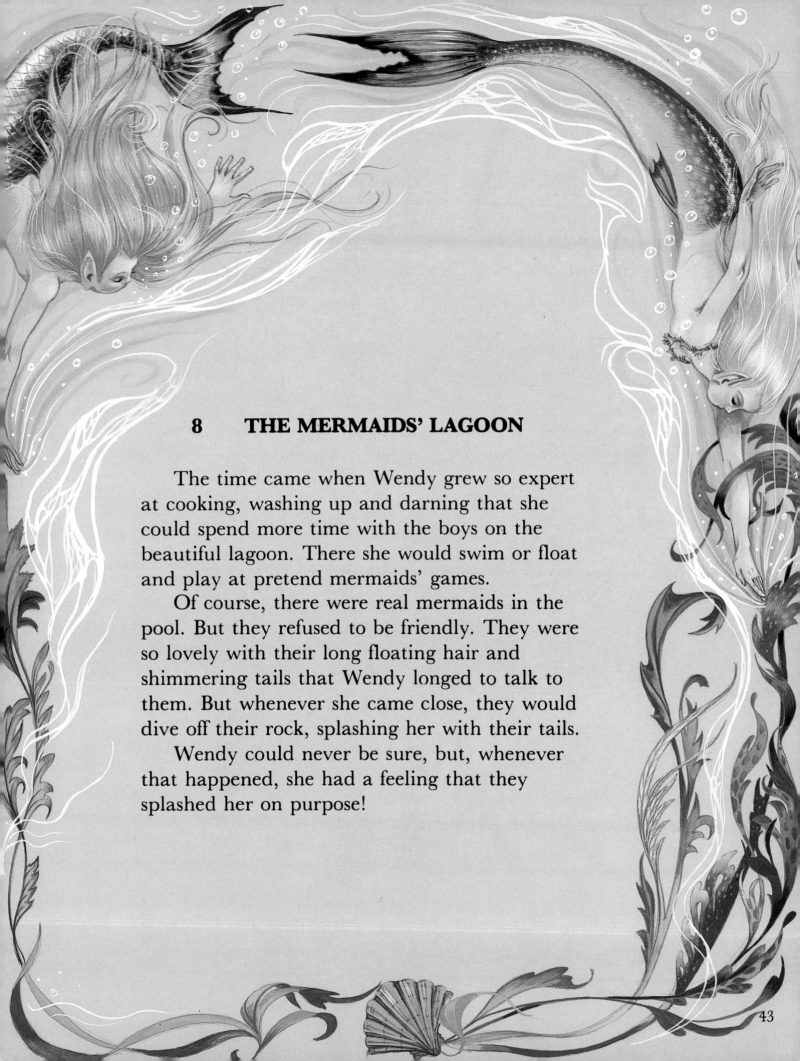

8   THE MERMAIDS' LAGOON

The time came when Wendy grew so expert at cooking, washing up and darning that she could spend more time with the boys on the beautiful lagoon. There she would swim or float and play at pretend mermaids' games.

Of course, there were real mermaids in the pool. But they refused to be friendly. They were so lovely with their long floating hair and shimmering tails that Wendy longed to talk to them. But whenever she came close, they would dive off their rock, splashing her with their tails.

Wendy could never be sure, but, whenever that happened, she had a feeling that they splashed her on purpose!

One of their favourite rocks was called Marooners' Rock and it was here that Wendy brought the boys one summer day. The rock wasn't much bigger than their own great bed but the boys knew how to fit themselves on to it.

Wendy was busy sewing when a change came over the lagoon; the sun went in and it suddenly grew dark and forbidding. The boys had fallen asleep and Wendy did not wake them even though she could hear the sound of muffled oars. So it was just as well that Peter had come with them that day!

Suddenly Peter, who seconds before had been asleep, was wide awake. He sprang to his feet and shouted, "Pirates! Pirates! Dive everybody!"

Instantly awake, the boys gathered themselves together and obeyed. Now the lagoon seemed deserted as one by one the boys disappeared beneath the waves.

Peter and Wendy, who were close to the rock but out of sight, watched as the boat drew nearer.

"It's the pirates all right," Peter whispered. "That's Smee and Starkey and their captive is Tiger Lily!"

"Who is Tiger Lily?" Wendy asked softly.

"Daughter of the chief of the redskins," Peter told her. "They're going to leave her to die on the rock!"

As he spoke the two pirates, who were no sailors, crashed their dinghy on the rock and Smee swore loudly. Then he shouted "Come, let's hoist her on the rock!"

This was quickly done, and Wendy stifled a scream. Then she heard Peter laugh softly and to her amazement he began to shout, in a perfect imitation of Hook's voice, "Ahoy there, you lubbers! Set her free!"

Clearly the two pirates were dumbstruck at hearing Hook's voice, but so terrified were they of their captain that they cut the girl's bonds and set her free.

Before Peter could give vent to one of his triumphant conceited crows, the shout, "Boat ahoy!" rang across the lagoon.

"That's Hook's voice," Peter whispered. "He must be in the water and making for the boat!"

They had not long to wait before they saw Captain Hook haul himself into the dinghy. The picture of misery, he began groaning aloud. "We're undone, lads! The boys have got a Wendy mother. With a mother to watch over them it's curtains for us . . . ."

"It needn't be," said Smee after a pause. "We could kidnap the boys and put an end to them. Then we could make their Wendy mother our mother . . . ."

Hook's wicked face lit up. "Capital!" he cried. "Now then lads — let's be on the rock for a last glimpse of that pesty princess and we'll begin making plans . . . ."

"But captain," Starkey protested, as they scrambled on to the rock, "We let her go — on your orders . . . ."

"Brimstone and treacle!" Hook thundered. "You did what?"

"It was your voice and no mistaking," Smee put in.

Hook raised his fearsome claw as if he would strike him down and then thought the better of it. And while he hesitated, Peter Pan's voice rang out, "Tiger Lily is free — and it was me who set her free!"

No doubt about it — Peter was spoiling for a fight. And so, too, was the captain. With a loud curse, he dived into the lagoon, swimming in the direction of Peter's teasing voice.

It was not in the water, but on the slippery rock that they finally met. Hook returned there to catch his breath and Peter, scaling it on the opposite side, returned for the same reason. Neither knew the other was coming until suddenly they met face to face!

And, after all, there was not much of a fight for Hook treacherously used his claw in a violent upward movement which took Peter by surprise. Seeing he was wounded Hook was ready to finish him off. But before he could deal the fatal blow, he heard the ticking of the crocodile and made off in a dreadful panic!

Thankful for his escape, Peter used the last ounce of his strength to drag the fainting Wendy on to the rock and then lie down beside her, knowing that the water was rising and that they would soon be drowned.

"Do you think we could swim or fly as far as the island?" Wendy asked, when she came to her senses.

"No," said Peter. "I am too much weakened by Hook's claw. But you must try, Wendy. You must . . . ."

"I couldn't," Wendy protested in a feeble voice, and she shut her eyes again.

As they sat there, close together, something brushed against Peter so gently that he was scarcely conscious of it or what it could mean to them. Suddenly he exclaimed, "Why, look, Wendy, it's that kite Michael made. It must have broken free!"

The next moment Peter had seized the kite's tail and was pulling it towards him. "It can't lift two," he said. "But it can lift you, Wendy." And he tied the tail around her despite all her protests. "Good-bye, Wendy!"

Then he pushed her out from the rock and she was soon carried out of his sight. Now he was alone in the lagoon. The next moment he was standing tall on the rock, and there was a brave smile on his face as he gallantly awaited death.

9   THE NEVER BIRD

As the waters rose higher and higher Peter could hear the sound of tiny bells which told him that the mermaids were shutting the doors of their coral caves. They would stay at home until it was warm and sunny again.

Gazing straight ahead, suddenly Peter noticed something very odd out in the lagoon. Something out there was fighting desperately against the rising tide. It couldn't be just a big sheet of paper! No — it was the Never bird and she was making valiant efforts to steer her floating nest in the direction of the rock. He could see, by the way she made her wings work, that it was taking nearly all her strength to guide her strange craft towards him. And he saluted her courage.

When at last she was close enough to the rock she called out, "I have come to save you! I want you to get into the nest . . . ."

But Peter was so tired and weak from the wound he had received from Captain Hook's terrible claw that he could scarcely understand what the brave Never bird was telling him.

It soon became clear to the bird that she was failing to make Peter understand and she grew irritable and began screaming at him. It is a well known fact, of course, that Never birds have very short tempers!

"You stupid, dunderheaded little jay," she screamed, "why don't you do as I tell you?"

Peter began losing his temper too, but the Never bird was quite determined to save him and, at last, she began trying to propel the nest as close to the rock as she dared. And then Peter understood and as she flew upwards, he leaned out as far as he could and pulled the nest with its two large white eggs towards him.

51

The poor Never bird could scarcely bear to witness the fate which awaited her two precious eggs and she hid her face in her wings as she hovered in the air. But Peter saw at once how he could save them. He had shared his vanishing rock with one of the pirates' old hats which had been fixed to a post. Now he saw a way of making use of it!

The hat with its broad brim was watertight and after making sure that it floated Peter transferred the eggs to it without breaking them!

The Never bird realised what had happened when she dared to look and she screamed her thanks as Peter climbed into the nest, hoisted his shirt for a sail and set out for home. And, do you know, even when Peter landed and beached his craft in a place where the bird could easily find it, she still preferred the pirate's old hat!

10   THE HAPPY HOME

Peter had saved Princess Tiger Lily's life and this made
the redskin tribe extremely friendly towards him and the
boys. When they suggested that they keep watch over the
underground home, Peter gladly accepted. He knew that the
pirates would attack soon and, besides, he enjoyed being
flattered by them and being called the Great White Father.

At night they sat above ground on guard. In the daytime
they refused to leave the home unprotected, which meant
that Wendy and the boys got quite used to seeing them and
saying "How-do" as they met.

Sometimes when she had all the boys at home and seated on their mushroom stools, Wendy would talk to them about the brave redskins and listen to their own stories about their adventures. This happened mostly when they were enjoying a make-believe meal. But then, as on this particular night, the boys began to quarrel among themselves and even make unkind remarks about Peter. Wendy didn't know how to stop them and she gave a sigh of relief when at last she heard Peter coming. He would soon make them behave!

Peter had brought gifts for the boys, thinking he was acting like a proper father — which would certainly please Wendy! He had heard the clock inside the crocodile chime the hour just as he reached home so he was able to tell Wendy the exact time which she always liked to know.

Wendy liked it best when Peter returned home after a day's hunting. They would sit on their own special stools in front of the fire and talk over all the important events of the day, and Peter would sometimes call her "old lady" because he thought mothers liked to be addressed in that way.

Of course Wendy often wished that Peter would act more like a proper father instead of a make-believe one. But Peter always said that real fathers had to be grown up and he never, never would grow up. And with that Wendy had to be content. Most nights ended with a wild pillow fight in which everybody joined.

Being the smallest, Michael often sat down on the floor with a bump as one of the pillows hit him. But he never cried because it was all such good fun, and he enjoyed watching the soft white feathers flying about.

Peter and Wendy sometimes seemed to be having a private battle of their own with the pillows. But it always ended in Wendy laughing and Peter begging for mercy which suited her very well!

The boys were often so excited by these nightly pillow fights that they refused to go to bed. And then Mother Wendy would put on her very cross grown - up voice and speak to them very sternly. "Off with you!" she ordered. "To bed, I say!" Everybody knew when it was time to obey Wendy and soon the boys would be in the great bed and waiting eagerly for their nightly story.

Wendy's stories meant so much to the children that they could not bear to go to sleep until she had told them at least one. Wendy knew this and was secretly pleased!

11 WENDY'S STORY

Knowing the faithful redskins were keeping watch overhead on this night Wendy settled down to tell the boys a very special story. "There was once a gentleman," she began, and was immediately interrupted by Nibs who muttered, "I wish he had been a white rat!"

Wendy paid no attention. "This gentleman's name was Mr. Darling," she said, "and his wife was Mrs. Darling."

"I know them!" John burst out, just to show off in front of the others.

"They had three children," Wendy went on, "and a dear, faithful nurse called Nana. But one day Mr. Darling was angry with Nana and chained her up in the yard, and the children flew away . . . ."

"That's a splendid story," said one of the boys.

"I haven't finished yet," said Wendy. "They flew away to the Neverland where lost children are . . . ."

"Did they ever go back?" another of the boys asked. "I expect they did even though we didn't."

"Well," said Wendy, "I think perhaps they did after years and years because their mother, Mrs. Darling, loved them so much that she could not forget them. You see, night after night, she went to the nursery and left the window open, hoping they would fly back into the nursery . . . ."

Suddenly John cried, "Wendy, let us go home!"

Before Wendy could say anything, Peter remarked quietly, "You are wrong about mothers, Wendy. Long ago I thought the same as you about my mother always keeping the window open for me. I stayed away for moons and moons and then flew back, but the window was barred. Mother had forgotten all about me and there was another little boy sleeping in my bed . . . ."

"Wendy, Wendy, don't listen!" John cried again. "Let us go home now. Let us go tonight!"

"Oh no! Not tonight!" the lost boys protested. "We don't want to give up our mother!"

Wendy looked at Peter. "Will you make the necessary arrangements?" she asked.

"If you like," he replied calmly, just as if he didn't care! But, of course, he did care though he wasn't going to show it!

Presently he left the room to give orders to the redskins above ground. They must be warned that Wendy and her boys would soon be making their way through the forest.

Wendy smiled just as if she didn't care about leaving Peter and their underground home. Then she bent down to comfort Michael in the basket at her feet.

"Don't worry, Michael!" she whispered. "The window won't be barred! Our mother loves us too much to bar the window against us!"

"If we are going at once,"
John cried, "We must get ready
for the journey!" And he sprang
out of bed.

Then little Michael scrambled
out of his basket and Wendy
began thinking about what she
would take for the long journey
back to their nursery.

The lost boys watched silently
as she began bustling about the
big room, gathering little items of
food which she thought might be
useful. Then, all at once, they
grouped themselves and began
advancing on her in a
threatening way.

"If you go, mother, things
will be awful!" one boy
muttered.

"Let's keep her prisoner!"

"Chain her up so that she
can't escape!"

Suddenly afraid, Wendy looked around at the angry,
resentful faces. Who among the boys would help her? Tootles,
of course! She held out her hands in silent appeal to him.

Tootles drew his sword. "Nobody minds me much!" he
cried. "But the first who does not behave to Wendy like an
English gentleman will feel the thrust of my sword!"

Peter returned and the boys saw at once that they could not count on his support when he told Wendy that he had asked the redskins to guide her through the wood. "I know flying makes you very tired," he said. Then he went on, "Tinker Bell will take you across the sea."

As he spoke the boys began looking so forlorn and miserable that Wendy's heart melted. "Dear boys," she cried, "if you will all come with me I'm almost sure I can get my father and mother to adopt you . . . ."

The boys turned to their leader. "Peter, can we go?" they asked in pleading tones, taking it for granted as Wendy did, that Peter himself would want to be adopted.

"You may please yourselves," Peter replied with a bitter smile. As the boys rushed away to get some of their precious belongings, he added, "I stay here!"

After Wendy and the children had said their good-byes to Peter who behaved with the greatest dignity, Tinker Bell darted up the nearest tree. No one followed her for it was in that instant that the pirates made their treacherous attack. They had broken all the rules of honourable warfare by launching their attack in the night. The redskins, as they squatted above the children's home, wrapped in their warm blankets, were taken completely by surprise.

Suddenly, when moments before there had been silence, the air was filled with the clash of steel and triumphant shouts of the attacking pirates.

Wendy hid her terror as well as she could but the boys made no pretence of being brave as they cowered on the floor. Only Peter seized his sword, the thrill of battle in his eyes.

Above ground the battle waged fast and furious. Recovering from their first shock at the surprise attack, the redskins uttered their war-cry and launched themselves forward to meet the pirates. A dozen or so of the stoutest warriors grouped themselves around brave Tiger Lily, prepared to go to their happy hunting ground in her defence.

Others, still bewildered by the treachery of their enemy, left themselves in full view of the attackers and were fatally wounded.

But not all the redskin braves conducted themselves badly. One of the pirates fell to the tomahawk of the terrible Panther, who finally cut a way through the fighting men with Tiger Lily and a small remnant of the tribe.

Hook himself took no part in the fighting but stood some way apart, breathing heavily and making no attempt to hide the pleasure he took in the slaughter of the redskins. He knew, of course, that the night's work was not yet over, for it was not the redskins he had come to destroy. It was Peter Pan he wanted, Peter Pan and Wendy and their band, but chiefly Peter Pan.

Hook's hatred for Peter Pan was something to be marvelled at. But it was not only because Peter had tossed a bit of him to the crocodile. No, it went deeper than that! Probably Hook himself did not fully understand the true reason for it but, if you had asked him, he might have said that it was most likely because he could not stand the conceit of the boy and his impudence!

While Peter lived Hook knew in his black heart that he would have no peace. And, as he stood there, legs wide apart, Hook began savouring the moment when he would have Peter in his power.

Meanwhile the battle still raged on, some of the redskin warriors putting up a fight which astonished the pirates who held them in small regard at the best of times. And here, it must be admitted that most of Hook's pirate dogs (as every now and then they took time off to wipe their cutlasses) had no intention of laying down their own lives in their captain's cause!

Hook's deep-set eyes, dark with hatred and the thoughts of revenge, glinted evilly as the last of the braves were defeated, and as suddenly as it had begun the battle was over!

One or two of the pirates went over to the mouths of the trees to try and discover what was going on in the underground home. They heard little Michael ask how they would know who had won the battle. And, alas, they heard Peter's reply: "If the redskins have won," he told them, "they will beat the tom-tom. It is always their sign of victory!"

This conversation they reported to their captain. By chance Smee had found the tom-tom and was at that very moment sitting on it. Imagine his astonishment when Hook signalled to him to beat the tom-tom!

Being simple-minded, Smee could not understand the order until, all at once, the meaning of it became clear. And the dreadful cunning which lay behind the order filled the pirate with boundless admiration.

He cast a look of warm approval at his clever captain before beating upon the drum.

While the tom-tom sounded, Hook nodded his head, well pleased with himself, for as his men listened they heard the boys cheering wildly. And then Peter's cry rang out, "The tom-tom! An Indian victory!"

Hook then took the centre of the stage directing the ruffians as if they were so many actors. In a low voice and with a wave of his iron claw he set one man to each tree and the others to hold themselves in readiness to grab any of the boys who managed to get away.

Greatly relieved that they would not be ordered to squeeze themselves into the tree hollows, the pirates obeyed promptly, smirking and rubbing their hands at the idea of capturing Peter and his band without so much as a tussle.

13   DO YOU BELIEVE IN FAIRIES?

The full horror of what happened next can be told in a few words.

One of the first boys to climb out of his tree was Curly. He came out straight into the arms of one of the biggest and boldest of the pirates, Cecco by name, who flung him to Smee, who flung him to Starkey, who flung him to—but why go on?

Curley was tossed like a bale of cloth from one pirate to the next until, finally, he fell at the feet of the blackest, most notorious pirate of them all, the evil Captain James Hook.

Here it must be admitted that for once the pirates seem to be enjoying themselves hugely as the game of "toss-the-boy" went on in an organized way under the eagle eye of their captain.

The same fate awaited all the boys plucked from their
trees. Only Wendy was accorded a different kind of
treatment. With mock politeness Hook raised his hat to her
and offering her his arm, escorted her to the spot where the
boys were being tied up.

Then, to prevent them taking flight, Hook ordered they
be bent double with their knees close to their ears and trussed
up like chickens. But how to convey the prisoners to his ship?
Hook's keen brain solved the problem. "Bundle them into the
Wendy house," he ordered. "And carry it on your
shoulders!"

When the children were shut inside the Wendy house
several of the strongest pirates hoisted the little house on their
broad shoulders and set off through the forest.

As soon as the strange procession was out of sight, Captain Hook made for one of the tree openings which was wider than the others. By dint of squeezing and pushing he could just manage to slide down and so enter Peter's underground home. And it was Peter Pan, his arch enemy, that Hook was so desperately pursuing!

"Now he is mine!" Hook told himself, as he stepped into the tree. Once at the foot of the shaft his eyes grew accustomed to the dim light and his eager gaze fell immediately on the bed where Peter lay fast asleep, one arm dropped over the edge.

Silently gloating, Hook took a stealthy step forward only to be brought to a stand-still by a stout door which barred his way into the big room. Then, he realised that he had been peering at Peter over the top of this ill-fitting door and there was no way he could reach the catch to release it.

Was Peter going to escape him after all? Hook trembled at the very thought. Suddenly the sight of Peter's medicine on the mushroom stool by the bed gave him a brilliant idea. With shaking hand he took from his pocket the deadly death-dealing drug he always carried about his person to administer to himself in the event of capture. And pushing his arm through the opening he let fall five drops of the fatal drug into Peter's cup.

"It's done!" Hook muttered, and with one final gloating glance at his victim, he wormed his way up the tree.

Peter slept on until the light went out, leaving the room in darkness. He was awakened only by the coming of Tinker Bell who could scarcely remain still as she told him all that happened and how Wendy and the lost boys had been taken to the pirate ship.

"I'll rescue them!" Peter cried, springing up. "But first I will take the medicine Wendy left for me. That would please her!"

"No! Don't touch it!" Tink screamed. And, as Peter raised the cup to his lips, with one lightning movement Tink got between his lips and the draught and drained it to the dregs. She reeled in the air and then spun gently round and fluttered down. "I'm dead Peter!" she whispered.

"You must not die, you can't die!" Peter shouted. "I won't let you!"

But Tinker Bell's light was growing fainter and fainter and now her voice was just the merest whisper. "There is only one way to save me, Peter. Children everywhere must believe in fairies . . . ."

Peter flung out his arms. "Do you believe?" he cried to all the invisible children of the world. "Tell us you believe!" And somehow the answer came back, loud and clear, "Yes, yes, we believe in fairies!"

"Clap your hands then," Peter shouted again, "and Tinker Bell will hear . . ."

And Tinker Bell did hear! Her light grew stronger and stronger and when she spoke she sounded like her old self again. She would have kept Peter at her side but he insisted that he must set out at once to rescue Wendy and the boys.

Soon, fully armed, he left the underground home and set off through the wood, pressing forward in redskin fashion through the silent night. The crocodile passed near to him, but not another living thing, not a sound, not a movement, disturbed the deadly hush of the wood.

14   ABOARD THE PIRATE SHIP

Meanwhile, on board the *Jolly Roger*, which lay at anchor in Kidd's Creek, Captain Hook paced the deck deep in thought. The Wendy mother and the lost boys were safely aboard, prisoners! And Peter was dead!

Presently, the pirates broke into their dreadful ditty, "*Avast belay, yo ho, heave to, A-pirating we go . . . .*" They were always more at ease when aboard the *Jolly Roger*, taking pride in her reputation for being the cannibal of the seas. And cannibal she most certainly was, and filthy dirty, her decks never washed from one month to the next!

At the sound of the noisy tuneless singing, Hook scowled and thundered out an order. Smee immediately set out the barrels on which his captain liked to sit and use for playing patience. Then Hook asked, "Are all the children chained so they cannot fly away?"

"Ay, ay," came the answer.

"Then hoist them up."

The wretched prisoners were dragged from the hold, all except Wendy. Hook stared at each one in turn as he fingered his pack of cards. "Six of you walk the plank tonight, but first I have room for two cabin boys. Which of you is it to be?"

"Don't irritate him unnecessarily," had been Wendy's instructions in the hold, so one or two of the boys shook their heads. And Tootles said gently that he didn't think his mother would like him to be a pirate.

Suddenly John asked, "Shall we still be respectful subjects of the King?" And Hook hissed through his teeth, "You would have to swear 'Down with the King'."

"Then I refuse," said John. "Rule Britannia!"

"Rule Britannia," squeaked some of the others, and the infuriated pirates tried to get them to shut their mouths, as Hook roared, "Get the plank ready!"

The boys grew pale and began to tremble when they saw the two pirates with the plank. But they tried to look brave when Wendy was brought up on deck to be a witness to their dreadful fate.

"Are they to die?" Wendy asked, with a look of such scorn and contempt that Hook found himself avoiding her eyes.

"They are!" he snarled. "And you will watch every one of them perish beneath the waves!" Then he turned to Smee and ordered him to tie Wendy to the mast.

Now, it must be admitted that not one of her children gave her a glance as she was tied to the mast. Their eyes were fixed on the plank and their thoughts were on that last short walk they must take before hitting the water.

Hook smiled darkly at them and took a step towards Wendy. He meant to make sure that her face was turned in the direction of the boys. She must watch each one walk the plank in turn. He would not spare her!

But the evil captain never reached her. Something stopped him dead in his tracks. It was the one sound on earth he dreaded — the tick tick tick of the crocodile!

Caught in the middle of one of his mocking salutes to Wendy as he advanced towards her—the sudden change that came over him was terrible to witness. The bold captain fell on his knees, as he staggered away. Then he let out a piercing shriek, "Save me! Save me!"

His men gathered round him and he whispered hoarsely, "It's the crocodile! She's after me and drawing close . . . ."

And with that he crawled, like a stricken animal among them, cowering low to the deck in the vain hope that when the hungry monster hoisted itself aboard it would not see him.

Was it a vain hope? The persistent tick tick tick grew louder and ever closer as the dismayed pirates waited in hushed silence . . . .

15 "HOOK OR ME THIS TIME!"

The astonishing spectacle of the bold captain hiding among his sea-dogs put fresh courage into the doomed boys and they rushed to the ship's side hoping to welcome the crocodile aboard!

Instead, they were in for the surprise of their lives. No crocodile was coming to their aid — it was Peter, magnificent, gallant Peter!

Long afterwards Peter told the boys how on meeting the crocodile in the wood he had decided that one day he might put its ticking to good use. "The old crocodile was silent," he had explained, "And that told me its clock had finally run down, so I felt free to use its ticking for my own purpose when I saw a way of getting close to the captain."

It was the work of a moment for Peter to clamber aboard unseen, for the pirates were fully occupied shielding their terrified captain, that is, all but one, the quartermaster who kept watch along the deck.

Peter struck out with his dagger, and John clapped his hands on the stricken pirate's mouth to stifle his last groans before four of the boys cast him overboard.

In a flash Peter vanished into the cabin while the boys took up their positions on deck, acting as if nothing unusual had happened. They were not a moment too soon for Smee suddenly cried, "It's gone, captain! All is quiet again! The crocodile has gone!"

Slowly Hook pulled himself to his feet, all the time listening intently. When he heard no sound of ticking, he drew himself up to his full height and cried, "Now for Johnny Plank. Prepare the prisoners!"

And to put fresh terror into the boys' hearts he broke into a frenzied dance, grimacing and singing,

"Yo ho, yo ho, the frisky plank,
You walks along it so,
Till it goes down and you goes down
To Davy Jones below!"

At the end of his cruel ditty, he enquired with deceptive tenderness, "Now then, do you wish a touch of the cat before you walk the plank?"

And the boys fell on their knees, begging for mercy.

Hook smiled broadly. "Fetch the cat, Jukes," he ordered, turning to one of the pirates. "It's in the cabin!"

The boys exchanged knowing glances. Peter was in the cabin! A sudden terrifying scream came from the cabin, followed by an ear-splitting crowing sound which comforted the boys but did nothing for the nervous pirates. All were waiting for Jukes' appearance with the cat and when he did not appear Hook, with a wave of his iron claw, sent a reluctant Cecco into the cabin.

He emerged, gibbering and terrified. "Jukes is dead, stabbed!" he burst out, "and there's something awful in there — it's the thing you heard crowing; it's the death-dealing doodle-doo! I've heard of such things!"

Hook, visibly shaken, was yet determined to send his men one by one into the cabin to solve the mystery; and one by one they refused for each, being highly superstitious, was now desperately afraid.

At last Hook, out of patience, grabbed a lantern and, raising his claw with a menacing gesture, shouted, "I'll bring out that doodle-doo myself!"

His return was unexpectedly quick. "Something blew out the light," he explained. "I saw nothing!"

Meanwhile as the pirates conferred together, Peter slipped from the cabin and began cutting Wendy's bonds. "The boys are organized to fight," he whispered, knowing that she would not require time-wasting explanations. "Now you must join them whilst I take your place by the mast. Leave the cloak so that I can wrap myself in it as a disguise."

Then as Wendy slipped away silent as a shadow, Peter took a great, deep breath and began to crow.

Terrified, several of the pirates rushed towards the mast, shouting, "Fling the girl overboard! She's the Jonah among us! Put an end to her!"

It was then that Peter flung off his cloak to reveal who had been their undoing. Hook himself stood there stunned into silence at the sight of his old enemy, alive and seemingly full of high spirits!

"Down, boys, and at them!" Peter's voice rang out before Hook had time to pull himself together, and in another moment the clash of arms was heard all over the ship.

Now it is more than probable that the battle might have gone the pirates' way for the boys were armed with only what weapons they could easily pick up. But the pirates themselves were totally disorganised and their nerves raw and shattered by all that had been happening.

Hook fought like a tiger at bay, seemingly a match for three or four of the boys at one time. Again and again they closed in on him, only to be driven back.

At last a voice rang out with an order which they dare not disobey, "Put up your swords, boys," cried Peter. "This man is mine!"

So it was that Captain Hook came face to face with Peter Pan. And with only the briefest exchange of insults, the two fell upon each other. Peter, the superb swordsman was pitted against another superb swordsman, who did not scruple to use his hook when cornered.

A lucky thrust from Peter's sword finally pierced the Captain's ribs and at the sight of his own blood, the pirate lost all stomach for the fight. He staggered back and as Peter advanced towards him, he climbed on the bulwark and fell with a mighty splash into the water where the ever-watchful hungry crocodile was waiting for him!

It was the end of the pirates' rule, for the few who did not perish on board the *Jolly Roger* that day were captured by the redskins when they swam ashore.

16   THE RETURN HOME

After the battle Peter summoned his band of fighting men to announce his plans. They would all put on pirates' clothes and act under his orders.

The boys cheered loudly at this and prepared themselves for a long voyage under their gallant captain. Only Wendy thought wistfully of home and the nursery window which she hoped was still unbarred.

Little did she know that the only change in the night-nursery was that between nine and six Nana's kennel was no longer there. Every morning it was carried with Mr. Darling in it to a cab which took him to the office, and he returned the same way at six. By living in the kennel, Mr. Darling hoped to show that he alone took all the blame for the loss of his beloved children.

But to return to Wendy — at last she told Peter that she was going home. "Nothing has changed," she said. "And I believe the lost boys are coming with me!"

Too proud to persuade her to change her mind, Peter pretended that he did not care, but already he was forming a plan. He and Tink would fly quickly to the nursery and bar the window so that Wendy and her brothers would have to return to the Neverland!

When Peter and Tinker Bell reached the nursery they flew in through the open window. Mrs. Darling had been sitting at the old day-nursery piano. Now she had fallen asleep, her gentle face still wet with tears.

"Quick Tink," Peter said in a whisper. "Bar the window. You and I will get away through the door. When Wendy comes she will think her mother has barred the window against her and she will fly back to the Neverland with the others."

This was the trick Peter had meant to play all the time but when he saw just how sad Mrs. Darling's face looked, he suddenly felt ashamed.

"It's no use, Tink," he said. "I can't bar the window after all. Let them have their silly mother. We don't want mothers, do we?"

So Wendy, John and Michael found the nursery window open after all, which was perhaps more than they deserved! As they landed on the floor, Michael looked bewildered for already he had almost forgotten everything about his life at home. "Have I been here before?" he asked timidly.

And John said almost crossly, "Of course you have, stupid! There's your old bed."

Then Michael discovered his father in the kennel and did not recognise him so it was just as well that Mr. Darling was sound asleep!

As for Wendy and John, they could not understand why their father had chosen to sleep in Nana's kennel but they were too excited to be bothered by it.

"Let's get into our own beds," Wendy suggested, "and be there when Mother comes into the night-nursery."

Presently Mrs. Darling woke up and went into the night-nursery to find out if her husband was still asleep. The children waited for her cry of joy but it did not come. She saw them in their little beds but she could not believe they were real! She thought it was just another of her dreams!

The children could not understand this and they grew frightened. Then Wendy jumped out of bed, followed by her brothers. "Mother," she cried, "it's me!"

And John cried, "Mother!" And little Michael shouted, "It's me, it's me!"

Mrs. Darling stretched out her arms and the children ran to her and she hugged and kissed them as if she would never let them go.

After a while, Wendy managed to gasp, "The window was open after all — I said it would be!"

And Mrs. Darling smiled her gentle, tender smile as she told her how never for a moment had she forgotten her dear lost children.

It took a long time for Mr. Darling to recover from the shock of seeing his children again. And Wendy held back until he was recovered before she finally told him about the lost boys.

"They are waiting under the lamppost," she said.

In fact the boys were counting up to five hundred before entering the house.

They stood in front of Mrs. Darling with their hats off, and wishing that they had not been wearing their pirate clothes. They said nothing but their eyes asked her to have them!

Of course Mrs. Darling said at once that she would be happy to have them. But Mr. Darling could not help thinking about the extra mouths to be fed. It was quite clear that he considered six rather a large number.

Peter and Tinker Bell waited just long enough for the lost boys to be adopted.

"Goodbye, Wendy," he called, as he hovered in the air.

"Oh dear, are you going so soon?" Wendy cried, leaning out of the nursery window. "You don't feel that you would like to talk to my parents about me?"

"No," said Peter. "That would be like growing up!"

Then Mrs. Darling called from inside the room that she would gladly adopt Peter with the others. But Peter only smiled. "I don't want to grow up and be a man," he said. "Now I'm going back to the house we built for Wendy."

Of course Mrs. Darling could see how much Wendy cared about the little house, and so she said quickly, "Wendy can spend one week in every year with you and help with the spring cleaning!"

Wendy wished it could be longer, but Peter seemed satisfied as he flew away.

At the end of the first year Peter came for her and they had a lovely spring cleaning in the little house in the tree tops. But the next year he forgot and Wendy didn't mind as much as she thought she would. After that she was growing up so fast that sometimes she forgot all about Peter and the Neverland.

So too did the lost boys — lost no longer but all preparing to be important men of business or wise men of the law!

It was really quite astonishing how the years rolled away and how everything seemed to change. Michael became an engine-driver and John grew a beard and got married. Wendy got married too!

In time Wendy had a daughter called Jane, and sometimes Wendy told her about Peter Pan and how she slept in the very nursery visited by Peter long, long ago. And sometimes, with great cunning, Jane would persuade her mother to tell her more and more stories about Peter and how the little Wendy house needed spring cleaning once a year.

"He won't ever come back," Wendy said once. "He's forgotten all about me!"

But one night Peter did come back. When he found Wendy grown up and the mother of a little girl, he gave a cry of pain.

"I can't help being grown up," Wendy told him, but Peter went on crying until, suddenly, the little girl in the bed sat up.

"Why are you crying?" she asked. "I know who you are! You're Peter Pan, and I've been waiting for you!"

When Peter took out his pipes and began to play, Jane climbed out of bed. "I can fly, you know!" she laughed. And as Peter rose in the air, she rose with him and together they made for the open window.

"It's only for the spring cleaning," Jane called to Wendy. "I'll be back soon!"